How Turtle Got His Shell

Susan Akass

Illustrated by Tania Hurt-Newton

Rigby

Once there was a turtle
who did not have a shell.
He lived next door to Parrot.
Parrot had a beautiful garden.

KEEP OUT

One day, Turtle was hungry.
He looked into Parrot's garden.
"I can see delicious fruit
and Parrot is asleep," said Turtle.

So Turtle went into Parrot's garden.
Turtle ate some berries
and he ate some mangoes.

Suddenly, Parrot woke up.
He saw Turtle in his garden.
"Stop thief!" he squawked.
Turtle tried to get away.

Parrot caught Turtle by the leg.
He took Turtle to his house.

"I am hungry!" said Parrot.
"I'll make some delicious turtle soup."
He put Turtle in a big bowl.
Then he looked in his recipe book.

Then Parrot went to get wood for the fire.

"I don't want to be soup," said Turtle.

He tried to get out of the bowl.

Turtle wiggled and wriggled.
The bowl wibbled and wobbled
and it toppled off the table.
The bowl landed on top of Turtle!

Just then, Parrot came back.

He could not see Turtle.

He could not see the bowl.

Then Parrot saw the bowl walk to the door.

Turtle was under the bowl!

"Stop!" squawked Parrot.

Parrot pecked and pecked at the bowl.

But he could not get Turtle out.

Under the bowl,
Turtle walked out of the garden.
"Stop! Stop!" cried Parrot.

Under the bowl,
Turtle walked into the sea.
"Stop! Stop!" cried Parrot.

Under the bowl, Turtle swam away.
And that is how the turtle got his shell.